Dear Parent:
Your child's love of reading starts here!

Every child learns to read in a different way and at his or her own speed. Some go back and forth between reading levels and read favorite books again and again. Others read through each level in order. You can help your young reader improve and become more confident by encouraging his or her own interests and abilities. From books your child reads with you to the first books he or she reads alone, there are I Can Read Books for every stage of reading:

SHARED READING
Basic language, word repetition, and whimsical illustrations, ideal for sharing with your emergent reader

BEGINNING READING
Short sentences, familiar words, and simple concepts for children eager to read on their own

READING WITH HELP
Engaging stories, longer sentences, and language play for developing readers

READING ALONE
Complex plots, challenging vocabulary, and high-interest topics for the independent reader

ADVANCED READING
Short paragraphs, chapters, and exciting themes for the perfect bridge to chapter books

I Can Read Books have introduced children to the joy of reading since 1957. Featuring award-winning authors and illustrators and a fabulous cast of beloved characters, I Can Read Books set the standard for beginning readers.

A lifetime of discovery begins with the magical words "I Can Read!"

Visit www.icanread.com for information
on enriching your child's reading experience.

W9-ATY-061

I Can Read Book® is a trademark of HarperCollins Publishers.

The Berenstain Bears and the Ducklings
Copyright © 2018 by Berenstain Publishing, Inc.
All rights reserved. Printed and bound in the United States of America by LSC Communications.
No part of this book may be used or reproduced in any manner whatsoever without written permission except in the case of brief quotations embodied in critical articles and reviews. For information address HarperCollins Children's Books, a division of HarperCollins Publishers, 195 Broadway, New York, NY 10007.
www.icanread.com

Library of Congress Control Number: 2017938992
ISBN 978-0-06-265456-4 (trade bdg.) —ISBN 978-0-06-265455-7 (pbk.)

18 19 20   LSCC   10 9 8 7 6 5 4 3 2
❖
First Edition

The Berenstain Bears®
and the
Ducklings

Mike Berenstain

Based on the characters created by
Stan and Jan Berenstain

HARPER

An Imprint of HarperCollinsPublishers

The Bear family visits Farmer Ben's farm.

They like to help feed the animals.

They feed the chickens.

They feed the pigs.

Down at the pond, the bears feed the ducks.

There is a mama duck and a papa duck.

The papa duck has a bright-green head.

It's time to go home.

"Good-bye, duckies!" say the cubs.

The ducks follow the Bears home.

"No more food, duckies!"

says Mama.

But the ducks don't want food.

They look around the yard.

Mama Duck pokes into the flower bed.

The ducks waddle away.

What were they looking for?

The next day, Sister goes out the

back door.

Is that a quack she hears?

She looks in the flower bed.

It's Mama Duck!

She is sitting on a nest.

Sister shows the nest to
the rest of the family.

"Mama Duck will lay her eggs here,"
says Mama Bear.

"We must not bother her."

15

The Bear family stops using the
back door.
They only use the front door.

They try not to make too much noise.

They don't want to scare

Mama Duck away.

The cubs peek out the window.

Papa Duck comes by.

He takes a turn sitting on the nest.

Mama Duck needs something to eat.

She goes back to the farm.

Mama Duck soon comes back.

She sits on the nest again.

The cubs watch her and watch her.

Won't those eggs ever hatch?

One morning, the cubs peek
out the window.

They hear peeping sounds.

The eggs are hatching.

There are ducklings!

Mama and Papa Duck lead
their ducklings.
They lead them in a line.
They lead them right across
the front yard.

UH-OH!

Mama and Papa Duck are leading
their ducklings toward the road!

Papa calls
the police.

The police come right away.

They stop the cars on the road.

Mama and Papa Duck lead their
ducklings down the road.
The police go in front.

Soon, they come to
Farmer Ben's farm.

Mama and Papa Duck lead
their ducklings to the pond.
They all jump in.
They are very happy.
Brother, Sister, and Honey
feed the ducks.
They are very happy, too!